I0452136

SPACE WARRIOR

GALACTIC FEDERATION SERIES – BOOK V

THE BOUNTY HUNTER
SUB- SERIES

C. A. Salo – Author, Owner & Publisher

eBook ISBN- 978-1-7368487-8-4

Print ISBN - 978-1-7368487-9-1

Cover design by: C. A. Salo

Edited by: Editing with Heart

Printed in the United States of America

OTHER WORKS
by C. A. Salo

Listed at the end.
With a sneak peek into:
The Dragon King & The Shadow
Book VI of the Galactic Federation Series 3rd book
of The Bounty Hunter sub-series

CHAPTER 1

"FATHER, WHAT ARE THOSE?" Malia asked, pointing to the two silver objects streaming through the sky.

"Those are Space Warriors. They come and take the bad ones away. Now lift your mask. The winds are picking up."

Malia rubbed her palm over her face, brushing her hair back. She hadn't thought of her father in years. Maybe coming back to Scurn III wasn't a great idea. "One more stop and then I'm gone," Malia muttered as she slung back her drink. Rising, she tossed a few credits on the counter, lifted her mask, and headed out into the windy afternoon.

Everyone in the system referred to the four planets around the giant star as the Desolate Expanse. Malia called them home. Unless you were born on one of them, you didn't stay. Hell, she didn't know why she came back, but as long as she was here, there was one person she would see.

*

"You should not have come."

Malia met the old woman's eye. "You're the only one I have left, my only family."

"Yes, but do you not listen to your guides? Malia," she sighed, shaking her head. "Coming back will be your death."

Malia's chin lowered to touch her chest. "Then it is my death. I am so tired, Aunt Tula. I cannot do this anymore."

"Tired means you are alive."

Malia followed her outside into the sunshine to the edge of the cliff.

"You came on the wrong day, Malia, but I suppose it is fate, as a family member should be present."

A twisting streaked through her stomach. "Present for what?"

"It's my time, Malia. Listen to your guides. They will keep you alive."

The crushed rock crunched beneath her boots as Malia ran for the edge, her hand skimming the material of her aunt's dress. "No!" Reaching down, she missed again. Wide- eyed, Tula smiled at her before closing her eyes. Her chest ached, heaving sobs and sounds Malia hadn't heard since her father passed. Fingers clenched the crushed rock and dirt beneath, her aunt gone from her sight. Now she was truly alone.

"Malia Bash'ar, I'm Commander Ruskin. You are charged with murder, smuggling, and theft according to the laws of the Scorpii galaxy. You will come with me to stand trial for these charges."

Malia turned her head enough to see him from the corner of her eye. "Go away, Space Warrior." Her words choked, wet trails through the dust covering her face.

"I will not repeat myself. You are tagged as armed and dangerous. I will shoot to kill."

Malia chuckled through her misery, sharp edges of the crushed stone biting into her flesh. "Good! Because I have nothing left!" Rising, she turned, her gaze meeting the reflective helmet he wore. Head turned slightly; her eyes closed as the hot wind blew over her. "Nothing." Her whispered words barely met his ears as she stepped back. "Let me make it easy for you, Space Warrior. All you have to do is bring my genetic material back." Malia pushed off the edge of the cliff, her arms going out as the wind rushed her back, neck-length hair flying up around her face. She could already feel the change in the air, the depleted oxygen as she plummeted down. The good thing about her planet was the intense drops in breathable air. She'd black out before she hit bottom.

Malia's eyes drifted open when her body jerked.

"Not today Malia Bash'ar," Ruskin said as he caught her.

"I did not, do it." Malia whispered before blackness ensued.

*

Nolan tossed his helm to Rubu. "Do me a favor and test the voice synthesizer."

"Did it falter?"

"Not sure. When the prisoner responded, she did not do what the charges state. It registered she spoke truthfully. By the book, Rubu."

"Yeah, no problem, Commander. I'll let you know as soon as I have the results."

Nolan nodded as he headed for the bridge.

*

"So she's innocent, huh?"

Nolan smirked at his first officer. "So, they all say. Once Rubu is finished running a diagnostic on my helmet, I am sure there will be a deficiency."

"And if not?"

Nolan turned, meeting his gaze. "What makes you say so, Taltz?"

"Come on, Nolan. Look who initiated the warrant. He's not exactly innocent."

"Until we can prove otherwise, our hands are tied."

"What if your helmet comes back as working in perfect order?"

Nolan's brow scrunched. "We do our job." Stepping to the side, he headed for his quarters. There was something about this mission, this female. The moment he stepped up to her on that cliff he knew she was not the cold-blooded murderer made out in the warrant, and he signed with her. His musk had released, and his canines lowered. Frakin' wonderful, just what he needed, an outlaw for a mate.

Sighing, he sat down, clicking the screen on in front of him. Nolan brought up the detention area, focusing on her cell. She still slept from the lack of oxygen, the trail of tears still noticeable on her pale cheeks. She had referred to him as Space Warrior. Each planet or planet cluster, like the four planets of Scurn, had its own name for his division. He liked hers.

*

His eyes whipped open; something had woken him. No sirens, so they weren't under attack. Running a hand down his face, his gaze went to the screen as the female prisoner gave the male in the next cell a nasty retort and hit the communicator just under his ear. "Hoy."

"Commander?"

"You're in the brig, correct?"

"Yes sir."

"What's going on?"

"The female woke up and as she was washing her face, the male prisoner commented on how he'd like to...tap her."

Nolan sighed. "Figured as much. I'm on my way. Make it known to the idiot that she's wanted for murder, play it up."

"Yes sir."

When Hoy stepped into the frame, Nolan rose.

*

"Come on, baby."

Malia turned, eyes narrowed. "I'll cut your dick off and shove it down your damn throat. Leave. Me. Alone." When he made a face, she rushed the clear shield between them and kicked. A smirk lined her lips when he stepped back.

"I wouldn't be messing with her, Sy," Hoy said as he approached. "She's the one Commander Ruskin brought in."

"Ruskin?"

"Yeah," he smiled. "Tracked her down personally. This one here, she's wanted for murder."

Malia blinked slowly when the guard winked at her.

"The Commander put finding Drago on hold to go after her, so if I were you Sy, I wouldn't piss her off."

"Hey," Malia said as Hoy turned. "I want to see this, Commander Ruskin."

"I'll see what I can do."

Malia turned, eyeing the cell she'd been tossed into. No escape, at least for now. If this Commander put everything on hold to come after her, maybe she could use that to her advantage; after all, he didn't fire on her when she jumped. It could be the amount of the bounty, but he'd have been better off, letting her meet her end and bringing back her DNA and proof of what was left of her body, much easier than dragging her all the way back here. Unless...unless he worked for Vultag. Her insides went completely cold.

"Bash'ar, the Commander would like a word with you. Turn around, hands behind your back and don't go trying to run; you're onboard a star ship full of bounty hunters. You'll get nowhere but beaten and bruised or dead. Understood?"

Malia nodded, turned, and lowered her hands behind her back. Yeah, she understood all right. After the first manacle was on, she whipped around, elbow rising and smacked the soldier right on the nose sending him reeling back. Turning she came up with her other hand, her fist landed hard on his temple and followed him down, grabbed his weapon and ran for the door as the male prisoner yelled for her to let him out.

Her nose flared, chest rose as she glanced around a corner. It wouldn't take the guard long to hit the alarm and ran onto a lift after someone had stepped off. "Flight bay."

"The flight bay is restricted to members of the Turas."

She snarled at the computerized voice. "Go to the level above the flight bay." When the doors opened, she peeked out, no one, odd. Stepping off the lift, her gaze flew up when the alarm sounded, and the computer announced a security breach. "Shit." Glancing around, Malia headed toward a grate and ripped it off, blood dripped from the sharp edges as she slid in, lifted the grate back into place and stopped as feet went running by. Her head lowered and chest rose as she breathed deeply. Malia turned, the tunnel was almost too small and grimaced as she crawled.

*

Sliding down the ladder, she stopped, eyes squinted as she peered out of a grate to see a shuttle. Damn, this will most likely end up with her dead. But dead or in prison for the rest of her life for something she didn't do, well that was a hard one. Getting away to finish gathering the proof she needed was utmost.

Malia grunted as she removed the grate. Lifting it up, she placed it to the side, before grabbing onto the side and lowered herself down. Sidling up next to the shuttle, her fingers ran over the pad. "Who in the frak locks shuttles on board?" A growl escaped, as she smacked the controls. "Damn it!" her eyes shifted to the left when a soft scrape sounded behind her and turned slowly to see ten men with weapons drawn and a large warrior in front of them. Her hand lowered a fraction of an inch.

"I wouldn't."

Malia met the leader's gaze, it had to be this Commander she heard about. "Whether I take my life, or you do, it's all the same Commander. Drawing the weapon she took from the soldier, her eyes widened, teeth gritted as ten beams came at her. She would not scream, she would not cry, eyes rolled back as her body jerked, all going dark. By the goddess, she'd be coming home to her ancestors soon.

CHAPTER 2

NOLAN GLANCED DOWN AS his captive moaned. She hadn't muttered a word when his men shot her, and that was impressive. "Good you're waking up." His brow arched as her lashes fluttered and met his gaze, "Malia Bash'ar, you're officially dead."

"Wh...what?"

"You were killed while trying to escape, your DNA and a vid log has been sent to the federation. That way it will get Vultag off your back until we have the proof he committed the murder he's blamed you for, and we'll fix it with the federation at a later date."

He liked how her emotions showed; she hadn't been so jaded, she'd lost her morals or sense of right, and her blue eyes, damn. Clearing his throat, he placed his hands behind his back as his dick went hard.

"Why?"

"What you said before you passed out on Scurn III. My helmet's voice synthesizer

had you speaking truthfully and that has been confirmed by my tech who troubleshooted it for me, and as we both know, Vultag is a menace, and this is not his first attempt at framing someone who pissed him off. So, Malia, what did you do?" His head tilted as she sat up on her elbow.

"I turned down his advances."

"Smart girl."

"I'm hardly a girl, Commander."

"Hmmm, yes. Well, for now you are confined here, it's not much, but better than the brig. My medical advisor will be in to see you shortly. Until she is satisfied with your health, you will be under her care. I will return after duty and escort you to dinner if you're feeling up to it, but for now, rest and enjoy not having to run for the first time in four years."

Nolan turned and headed for the door.

"Thank you."

He stopped as the door opened, turned his head, met her gaze out of the corner of his eye, and with a slight nod stepped through, the whisper of the door closed behind him. "If she needs anything, let me know."

"Will do, Commander."

Nolan nodded to the guard and headed to the bridge. What the hell was it with her that had his body acting like it hadn't just fulfilled itself on Rania the pleasure planet? Damn, he didn't need this or what has been shown to him. "Not now, just not now."

*

"You're looking grumpy. What's the matter, wasn't our guest happy to learn she's dead?"

Nolan narrowed his gaze as he met Taltz's. "I guess, she's still a bit out of it from all those stun beams."

"You're the one who said make it look good."

Nolan scowled as he lifted his hand reader. "What's the next job look like?"

"The Narrian Cluster is where we're headed and controlled by the Jykar mercs."

"Has our target been acquired?"

"Yes."

"Then let's not waste time." Rising, he met Taltz's gaze.

"Sir, Korth is in the vicinity."

"Good, maybe we'll run into him and take him without incident."

Taltz chuckled. "Yeah. All right, Commander."

"Hey, we can all have high hopes." Shrugging his shoulder, he stepped into his office off the bridge. "Computer open a high-security channel to Vestor Prime."

"Channel open, Commander. Vestor Prime coming online, now."

Nolan waited until his contact came on vid. "Vestor."

"Commander, while on your next mission, you'll be gathering some data. Please make sure that data makes it off world with you. Code Sevion."

"Yes ma'am."

"And Commander."

"Ma'am?"

"Stay safe."

"Thanks, Mom. I'll do my best."

"I know you will. I've also started an investigation into a problem in the Nutherian system."

The corner of his mouth lifted. "Have you now?"

"Yes, during our last council meeting, a Ditherian came forward with some information into a, off-hands crime leader named, Vultag."

"I've heard of him."

"Yes, I'm sure you have. We sent a team in to investigate and should hear back from them soon."

"Let me know what they find out."

"I will. Vestor out."

Nolan nodded as his mother disappeared. So, he had a meeting with Korth or whatever the hell his real name was. All he knew was every now and then he would bring intel back to his mother and from there, no clue. It had to be big, or his mother wouldn't ask, so it was most likely some black op she was working on with the federation, and she obviously read between the lines of his last missive. Damn, she was smart. No wonder she was a Prime. Stepping back onto the bridge, he met Taltz's gaze.

"And how is *The Prime* doing?"

"Well, and she says to stop calling her that when you talk to her."

"Come on, I have to mess Auntie anyway I can."

Nolan chuckled. "Yeah, because she's too smart for you."

"Shit, man. She's smarter than everyone on this ship."

"Most likely, and back to the mission."

"We will be within shuttle range of the planet in twelve hours. Ingot is ready to shuttle you and the team. Once Ingot drops you off, he'll take cover approximately two kilometers out, as we take the Turas behind the second moon and stay there until you call for pick up."

"Excellent. Have the team meet me in the mission chamber an hour before we depart."

"Already done. Sargent Donnas will be leading."

"Good choice, how's Edmunds doing?"

"Better, and happy to be out of the medical bay and away from Louris' eye." He smiled.

Nolan grinned. "I bet. He doesn't like to be told; he can't be on missions."

"Right, like all of us. But the hard part is waiting until Louris clears you for missions. I know I had a hell of a time, doing nothing. But she's a damn good medical advisor, knows her stuff."

"And won't put any of us back on duty until she knows we're one hundred percent." Nolan nodded. "All right, I have some work to catch up on, you have the bridge."

"Aye Commander."

Taltz grinned as they passed each other on his way to the lift. Damn him, Taltz knew him too well. Heading to medical, he lifted his head in acknowledgement when Louris lifted her hand motioning a moment.

"Yes Commander, how can I assist?"

Nolan liked her. She was beautiful, brilliant, and a hell of a bounty hunter if she had to fight. "Update on Edmunds."

"Edmunds' update was listed in my daily report."

"Right, and I want to hear it from you." He cocked his hip and leaned against the wall.

"He's healing well; as all men go, their bedside manner when injured is something to be desired, but he should be able to go on missions in several days after our next checkup."

Nolan grinned. "Bedside manner, really Louris?"

She snorted. "Oh, please Commander, you know as well as I, men are grumpier than a Volarian bear when not able to go on missions."

"True, and our newest guest?"

"What are we calling her, now that she is officially deceased?"

"I don't know. I haven't spoken with her about that yet."

"Uh-huh. Well to her physical assessment, she's fine, a bit sore, and some nerves are still sleeping, most likely from her recent encounter with ten stun guns. But she'll be fine. Now to her psychological, that's a bit undetermined. She's stable and not a threat to herself or anyone aboard this ship. She's mentally exhausted and torn down from Vultag and being on the run for four years, and of course her only living member just became deceased in front of her own eyes. I'd say she has some issues to work out, but who amongst us doesn't. Oh, and as she's from Scurn III, she'll show the mating signs by way of her eyes shimmering."

His brows furrowed. "Why say that?"

"Your musk. I noticed the odor the moment I stepped into the room."

His gaze narrowed as he met hers. "Not happening."

"I'm not understanding why?" Her head tilted.

Damn, she was so analytical. "Because it's a no."

"The signs are showing on your end. I'm sure she'll show them as well, and if the Gods have intended for the both of you to be mates, then why fight it?"

His gaze narrowed. She was not likely to stop on something she thought she had knowledge of. "Louris, I know your logical brain and eidetic memory can't process why I'd rather not take a mate. It's more personal and, stubbornness if that will help you understand."

"Mmmm, yeah, no it does not. The Gods are speaking, you need to listen before they smack you upside the head."

His brows furrowed.

"There's nothing wrong with her Commander. She's in her prime for mating, strong, and independent, someone I thought you would take a liking to."

"Her attributes, we are not discussing. Now back to Edmunds..."

"Edmunds will be released when I authorize him for duty and not a moment before."

His brows lifted, as did hers and he held her gaze. "I see."

"I'm glad you do, Commander. Now if we are finished here, I have work to see too."

"Of course." His left eye twitched as she walked over to her assistant.

"Want me to look at that?"

Damn it. "Nope." Turning, he stepped out, shaking his head. "Damn."

*

Malia turned as the door to her room opened. She could say they were quarters, more along the lines of a cell, without bars. She had a bed, privy and sink, so more along the lines of a solitary chamber. Her gaze met those of the Commander as he entered. "Commander."

"As Malia Bash'ar is deceased, is there another name you would like to go by, until 'we find you alive again?'"

"I've gone by several to avoid detection by Vultag's spies, I like Lia the best, I haven't used it overly much, so, yes, I believe it will be the best."

"And it's a part of your name, so you will react appropriately when someone calls it out."

"Right." She shifted her feet, she knew the last time he was here, she thought a musky odor emanated. "What planet are you from?"

"Paseon, why?"

Her gaze lowered to the left for a moment. "I see."

"Explain."

Her nostrils flared with the scent of his musk as she lifted her eyes, her sight changed slightly as an aura shone around him, as she met his gaze. "I'd like to know where my...signed mate is from." His gaze narrowed, arms crossed over his chest. "Trust me, it's not like I was looking for this to happen either. The questions are, what were you going to do with me, being dead and all, and what are we going to do about this?" her hand motioned to her eyes.

"Signing is an indicator not an absolute."

Her gaze widened as her sight returned to normal. "I see."

"You see what?"

"You're one of those, but that's all right, nothing like a shocker. So, tell me Ruskin, what are your plans for me? Keeping me here in this—cell," her hand motioned to the room around her. "Dumping me off on a planet or helping me finish finding the proof against Vultag to free me?" Arms crossed over her chest, she cocked a hip as she kept his gaze. "Somehow I believe it's the later."

"Don't play mind games with me. It will not work."

"Mind games?" she chuckled as she straightened up. "Is that what you think I'm doing? Because I've asked questions you don't want to answer? No Commander, I don't play mind games. I'm straight forward, and because you don't want to see what the Gods have shown you, don't take it out on me. I just want answers."

"Let's go eat."

Malia stepped toward him as he turned, and the door opened. Her eyes closed and Kegels contracted as her nostrils flared with the scent of his musk. Damn. Taking a seat beside his first officer, as he sat at the head and Louris sat to her right, she liked how they engaged. Ruskin had let everyone know she would be referred to as Lia, from now on, until they were able to clear her. Which surprised her to know his entire crew was on board with this, and it wasn't as formal as she would have thought, then again, they were all officers, except for herself.

"Lia, I'm Lieutenant Edmunds, can you tell me how you met Vultag?"

"Through an associate of his. I knew who Vultag was but did not know my employer was, under his thumb, until Vultag came for a visit."

"On Scurn III?"

"Yes."

"What did you do?" Louris asked.

"I assisted with the scheduling of personnel. I had only been there a full moon cycle before Vultag's first visit."

"How many times did he appear?" Nolan asked.

"Ah, if I remember correctly, three. I thought it was normal, but from what my superior said, it was not, and then I was called into my employers' office and Vultag cornered me. I turned him down. When he advanced again, I turned him down with my knee hitting his crotch. I ran out as my employer and superior ran in from his scream and told them I quit." She shrugged. "The next thing I know, I'm being accused of murder and he's pointing the finger."

"Your employer was the one to show up dead."

"Yes."

"Where is your former superior?"

Malia lifted her gaze to his. "I don't know. I've tried finding her, but she just disappeared. I don't know if she went into hiding or Vultag got to her too."

"It's something to look into. Edmunds, as you're still confined to the ship, why don't you start a search."

"Now, wait a minute." Louris started. "I haven't released him from medical yet."

Malia's gaze went from Ruskin, who was smiling to his head medical advisor.

"You let him out of the med bay, he's not going on a mission, he's staying on ship, in front of a panel searching down leads."

Damn, he had a great smile. Clearing her throat, she glanced over at Edmunds, who was grinning. "So, Lieutenant I'm available whenever you are to give you everything, I've been able to find. It's not much, but hopefully with your systems and broader access to information, we'll be able to deal with Vultag quickly."

"Sounds like a plan, after the morning meal then?"

"Now hold on you two," Louris said.

"Louris, I'm going to be sitting behind a panel. My fingers were not injured."

Malia lowered her gaze briefly, with a smile as he lifted his hand wiggling his digits, and glanced up to see Ruskin's gaze on her and held his until Louris started giving Edmunds a hard time.

"Louris, he'll be sitting on his ass. If you prefer, I can order him to do it in the med bay so you can keep an eye on him, if that will make you feel better."

Malia's gaze went quickly to Louris. "I promise, if he starts, failing, I'll make him stop."

Louris sighed. "I see I am not going to win this argument. Very well, then. While I will not make you sit in the med bay, Lieutenant, I will take Lia's word that if you start to feel ill, she will have you stop."

"Why is it you'll take her word and not mine?" Edmunds asked.

"Ha, because Edmunds, she's not a bounty hunter itching to get back into the action, and while she's been on the run for four years, she has taken exceptionally good care of herself. Well, except when ten stun guns nailed her."

"Hey, not on me. He said to make it look good."

The corner of Malia's mouth lifted as she held up her hand. "I still have numbness in my finger." And held up her middle one, grinning at Louris' look and Edmunds' wide gaze as Lieutenant Triplett belted out a laugh and shook her hand out as she lowered it. "So tomorrow after the morning meal, then. All my items were taken when I was brought on board. In those items was a small bag which holds personal care stuff. We'll need the brush. I have a reader hidden in the handle with all the information I've found." Her gaze went to Ruskin.

"I'll make sure your belongings are released to you after the meal."

"Thank you." She lowered her gaze as her Kegels clenched. Damn it. Why the hell did she have to be attracted to and have her signs show with someone who didn't want her? Just her luck in the way of her life. Oh well, maybe it was best not to get too close, after all; if they couldn't clear her, they'd have to arrest her, right? Shit, that would be something, and he couldn't be mated to a suspected murderess, he was a bounty hunter, that wouldn't be good for business.

Sighing softly, she sat there until Ruskin rose and motioned for her to follow him as they said their good nights to his crew and followed behind him. When she was younger, she prayed to the Gods for a mate strong enough to help her, to stand by her. Now, now, she wasn't sure she wanted one. What if she had to go on the run again? Nothing like your mate having to hunt you down.

"Are you all right?"

"Hmm, yeah."

"If you're still feeling the effects of the stunning, I can have Louris come look at you."

She cleared her throat as she stepped by him into her room. "No, I'm fine. I was just messing with Edmunds."

"Very well, then I'll have your belongings delivered within the hour. If there's anything you need, there will be a crew member on this level past the lift."

"Thanks." She didn't want to meet his gaze. One, because she didn't want to get close to him and two, because she didn't want him to see her eyes. They were shimmering and he'd already turned down the idea of mating, so why her body couldn't process that fact she didn't know. "I...I think I'll just go to bed."

"I'll be here before the morning meal to escort you down."

Malia nodded. "Thank you, Commander." After he left, she turned, her chest rose, breasts hitting her shirt as she met her gaze in the mirror. They were shining. "Damn it, stop." But nothing. They just shimmered back at her. This was not going to be easy.

CHAPTER 3

MALIA SIGHED AS SHE leaned back in the chair, her eyelids fluttering. "So, what do you think?"

"I think you're damn good. I don't know how you were able to secure this information on your own."

The side of her mouth lifted as she peeked over at him. "I hated every minute of it. Do you really think it's good enough to help me, though?" She met his gaze when he turned to her.

"You're kidding right? I'd say with what we have here, you're able to at least put that warrant on hold for an investigation to start, why did you think it wasn't enough?"

Malia shrugged. "I'm not sure what I need to clear me, I mean, I don't know how the federation courts work or who he's paid off and has in his pocket. On three, if you're guilty, we shoot you or let you honor your family and go to the expanse."

Edmunds nodded. "Yeah, I've heard the drops are quite intense."

"They are."

"Is that why you jumped, to bring honor back to your family in the eyes of the planet?"

Her gaze lifted, meeting his head on. "That and being emotionally exhausted, I guess."

"Was she your only family left?"

"Yeah. It's eerie, you know, being the only one, knowing when you die, your bloodline dies out with you."

"Unless you have children."

Malia snorted. "That's not in the near future, Lieutenant."

"Huh."

Malia turned to look at him, as he turned back to the workstation. "What do you mean by that?"

"Huh, oh nothing."

The corner of her lip lifted. "Don't give me that." And smacked his arm, meeting his gaze when he looked at her out of the corner of his eye.

"I've seen your signs."

"Huh." She said and turned to the workstation.

"Now, what do you mean by that?"

Malia looked at him out of the corner of her eye. "Not happening, Edmunds."

"Why not? The Commander's a great guy."

"Because he is one of those who does not believe."

"He sure as hell is!"

Malia turned, meeting his gaze. "Then it must be because I'm a wanted fugitive or he's just not attracted to me."

His brows rose. "Ah, I get it. He said not happening, didn't he."

"Something like that."

"Listen Lia, I've known the Commander for over twenty years. He does believe in the signs. He's had a few bad relationships, as I'm sure you have, before you had to run. I'm not sure what you know about our people, but know this: once a Paseonian finds their signed mate, it's a done deal. There's something in us that will not let us walk away."

Her gaze lowered with an indrawn breath. "I know it was a shock for me when the signs came. I wasn't expecting it. I can imagine the same for him, and you know besides the fact, I am wanted. Seriously Edmunds, what would he do if we mated, and we can't find the proof to free me? He'd have to turn me in or hunt me down, because I ran for not wanting him to have to go against the codes of being a bounty hunter." She sighed loudly as she stretched her legs out. "I don't know, there's so many unknowns, so many ifs. I can understand why he's holding back."

"That's why we need to work fast, and with the intel you've gathered, we're more ahead than you think."

"Really?"

"Ya, so let's get rolling Lia."

Malia grinned as she sat forward and started typing on the workstation's keyboard. "All right Edmunds, what's our next move?"

*

Malia smiled as they sat at the table for the evening meal. They were a happy lot, these bounty hunters, and not as stiff and formal or crazy and military like some she'd met. They didn't hide their faces to protect their identity. Paseon like Gruna and Du'Shara were warrior worlds, where most of their citizens were either in the military, bounty hunters, or mercenaries. Although Paseon was more open to trading to the federation unlike Gruna, they had more open ports and people knew you just didn't fuck around with them. Their laws were very harsh. Harsh but fair. She'd say they were more severe than three. They had a saying about Paseon: if you don't want to die, don't lie, steal, or murder. Their technology was advanced and knew when someone was lying, like the Commander's helmet when she uttered she didn't do it. If a Paseonian brought you to justice. It was known as factual because they'd have all the proof they needed to do so. She's also heard that because of how they ruled, Paseon was a peaceful planet. You could walk around free and not worry about someone coming up to rob or rape you. Paseon was also much more friendly to outsiders. Now Du'Shara and Gruna, on the other hand, well, they just smashed the shit out of you if you bothered them.

"What are you thinking about?" Nolan asked.

"Huh, why?" She met his gaze.

"You're smiling, and Louris just asked you a question."

Her eyes widened as she glanced down to the medical advisor, to see everyone smiling. "I'm sorry, I was wool gathering and didn't hear the question."

Louris chuckled. "I guess so. I asked how it was working with Edmunds."

"Huh, oh, fine, no issues. Why?"

"Didn't he bug the crap out of you to go on missions?"

"No, he didn't complain once."

"No shit, Why do you cry like a baby in my med unit then?"

Malia grinned as Edmunds chuckled.

"Because Louris, I'm bored just sitting in the med unit doing nothing. You can't expect grown men who are constantly active to just, stop."

The corner of her lip lifted. "You stop well enough when you're hit with a thermal cannon. Oh wait, that's what hit you and why you're on medical leave." she snorted.

"You'd be itchy too if you had to stop what you do every day until someone told you that you can go back to it."

"Yeah, I know. That's why I try to get you guys back in action as soon as I can, but that doesn't mean I'm going to let you go without being totally positive you're good to."

Malia smiled. "She has a point, Edmunds."

"Yeah, I know."

Nolan smiled. "So. When can he be released back to duty?"

"It's in my report." Louris answered.

"Yes, but I'd like to hear it from you."

Louris sighed. "I swear Commander, you don't read them at all."

Malia glanced up when a grin lit his face, her Kegels clenched, and she lowered her eyes as her sight changed, indicating they were shimmering.

"If I may, ahem, Lieutenant Edmunds, has progressed in all areas since his injury and may return to full time duty with the next moon cycle." Ruskin grinned.

"Then why do you ask me if you've actually read it?" Louris frowned.

"Because, like I said, I like to hear it."

"Hey Lia, you okay there?" Edmunds asked.

Lia glanced up at him with a frown. He was grinning, damn ass. "Yeah why? And you're blinding me with your smile." She noticed Nolan looked her way and made sure she turned her gaze quickly away from him. Damn, he'd probably be pissed and blame her if she let his crew know they were signed as mated.

"Just wondering. Hey Commander, I gotta say, she's good at getting info on the low down."

"Meaning?"

"Didn't you read my report?" he asked with a grin as Louris told him to shut up.

"Get to it Edmunds."

"She has everything we need to ask for a hold in the warrant and request an investigation into it."

Nolan's gaze narrowed. "I read that. What else would you want to go with it?"

"Having Vultag admit it again wouldn't hurt, especially if he's sober."

Nolan grunted. "No shit, Edmunds. Tell me something I don't know."

Lia met Edmunds' gaze when he stated he had an idea. "What kind of idea?"

"I have a friend who's a mercenary. Nolan is also good friends with him, who hates Vultag as much as the rest of us and may be willing to help us get that information."

"Which would entail what?" Her gaze flew to Nolan when a sharp 'no' came from him.

"She'd be safe."

"I said no."

Lia's gaze widened with his tone. "Am I missing something here?"

Louris sat forward. "The Commander doesn't want you in harm's way, because the both of you have signed as mates."

Lia gasped. "Oh, I, ah, um..."

"Louris." Nolan growled.

"What? It's true and everyone sitting here knows it. You cannot hide what the Gods have shown, so stop it."

Lia lowered her gaze, glancing up at Nolan from the corner of her eye. The muscle of his jaw clenched.

"This meal is over."

Lia's gaze followed him as he rose and left the silent eating hall, before turning to Edmunds. "So, what's your plan?"

Louris chuckled. "You've got gumption to go against what Nolan wants."

"This is my life we're talking about. I will do what it takes to prove my innocence. After all, I have no father and no mate, so I'll do what I want."

"You do realize pissing off the Commander is not a good idea," Edmunds replied.

"What I realize, Lieutenant, is he cannot have it both ways. He either sees what the Gods have shown and acts on it, or he does not. Either way, it's still my life we're talking about here." Rising she kept his gaze. "So, I'll meet you in the morning and we'll go over the details. I'm sure you'll have all the safety protocols down as well. Until then, good night."

Stepping out of the eating hall, her breasts rubbed against her shirt as her nostrils flared with the indrawn breath. "Boy, where did I get a set of silver balls?" she mumbled before taking off to her quarters.

*

Lia came around the corner, head down, reading the manifesto, and gasped when she was grabbed. Her gaze widened as she lifted her hand to fight, until she saw Nolan. "By the Goddess, what the hell, Commander? You scared the shit out of me."

"I said no."

"So that gives you a right to manhandle me?" Tucking the tablet under her arm, she kept his gaze, her nostrils flared with his musk. "You need to make up your mind. I understand not wanting a mate who is on the run. That wouldn't do well for your image. However, you will not, stop me from proving my innocence. Mated or not."

His brow arched. "Really?"

Her stomach rolled. "Y...yes, really." Her Kegels clenched with the uplift of his mouth.

"Silver, huh?"

Lia's lip lifted; her head drew back slightly. "Heard that, huh?"

"I hear everything."

"I call bullshit."

"Were you not pleasuring yourself last night?"

Her gaze widened as she stared at him.

"But yet you couldn't seem to find your pleasure."

Her gaze narrowed as she stepped back. The freaking smart ass. "What's your point?"

"Just saying."

"What? That because you're being an ass, I can't seek my pleasure without you. Yeah, that's fair. You want nothing to do with me, yet you take enjoyment in watching my pain. Thanks, Commander." Stepping back, she headed for her quarters. What a jerk. Slamming her hand against her thigh as the doors shut, she dropped on her bed, and tossed the tablet to the table.

She lay onto her back and looked up at the ceiling, her chest lowering with each sigh. What the frak did he want from her? Why say she died just to turn around and torment her? Shit, he could have done that with her still on the wanted list, instead of slamming her with ten stun guns. "Just so you know, I'm going along with Edmunds' plan! Whatever it is!"

"We shall see."

Her lip lifted at his muffled voice. So, he was standing outside her door. "Yes we shall, stalker!"

"Stalker your ass."

"Ha! Then what would you call yourself, who stands outside my door listening?" her head turned when the door slid open.

"My ship."

"Oh yeah, so that gives you the right to barge into my cell?"

His gaze narrowed. "Cell?"

"Just because I can come and go, we both know it's a holding room or whatever you want to call it. I know you have microphones and cameras here. I'm not stupid, Commander."

"I never thought you were, and just because Edmunds has a plan doesn't mean you have to jump at it."

"If it's a good plan, I will. I don't see Edmunds as the type to propose something that has a high chance of failure."

"He's not. I have all the faith in his abilities."

"Then why won't you let me do it?"

"Because you could be hurt."

"I've been hurt, I've been in pain. It lets me know I'm still alive." Swinging her legs over the edge, she sat up, keeping his gaze. "I don't understand you, Commander. You push me away yet speak of my wellbeing."

Nolan stepped forward so the door shut. "Listen, I wasn't looking or ready for the signs. I like my life as it is. I go when I want, stay out as long as I want and don't have to worry about someone else and their issues. Am I attracted to you? Yes. Would I love to put you against the wall and fuck your brains out? Yes. But that doesn't mean I want a mate. Signs or not, it won't happen."

Her head tilted slightly as her eyes lowered. "As you say, then. Have a good night, Commander." Her breath lowered; she kept her gaze on the floor as he opened the door and glanced up through watery eyes as the door closed. Never would she let him see her cry. Never.

CHAPTER 4

HER LIPS PRESSED AGAINST each other as she sighed. She'd been able to ignore Ruskin for the last week, or at the very least be cordial while sitting next to him for meals. But now, Edmunds was escorting her to the bridge. "Are you going to tell me what this is about?"

"You'll find out when the Commander tells you."

"Why can't you tell me?"

"Orders are orders, Lia, and he's the boss. It's his ship."

"Oh, so he owns the ship?" she snorted.

Edmunds grinned as he glanced back at her. "Actually, he does."

Lia sighed. "Figures." She stepped onto the bridge behind Edmunds, going to the right, she caught Taltz's gaze, before going into another room. She spotted Nolan the moment Edmunds moved. He didn't say anything until the doors closed.

"Lia, we're heading to a federation holding station."

"K," her shoulders and lip lifted. "So that's it? You could have had Edmunds tell me that." And met his gaze when he lifted them.

"You still would have had to go to a special area. There are a few on ship that do not allow any penetration of sound. So, no one can hear us."

She gazed at him as he stood and came around his desk. "Okay, so what's going on?"

"You are going to have to stay in my quarters until we depart the holding station and are away from the Halifax System."

"Ah, I'm sorry, what?"

"Unfortunately, my quarters, this office, and a few other select locations are the only rooms on board where your DNA sequence, life sign or brio cannot be detected, and as you should be aware, any federation station, especially a holding facility, will be scanning for all those items. So, from the time you leave this room until we are out of the Halifax System, you will have to stay in my quarters."

Her head tilted as she met his gaze. "This isn't a joke, is it?"

"No, and not something I look forward to either."

She snorted. "Oh, that I can see. Please tell me you have another bed chamber in your quarters."

"No."

"Fine, whatever, I've slept on the floor in worse places." She turned to Edmunds. "Let's go get me settled, shall we?" and headed for the door, walking ahead of him out to the lift, and silently entered.

"He tried staying away for as long as he could, but we have to turn our prisoners over."

"Why his chambers?"

"Because it's the only option for comfort."

"I've slept in a hole."

Edmunds chuckled and glanced over at her. "Lia, it won't be that bad."

"It is when it's stated how much you're not wanted."

"Is that why you've been giving him the cold shoulder?"

"He doesn't want a mate, Edmunds, you heard him, and he's stuck on the idea, so why go around and around with him when it's not going to happen, or be all in his face and prissy-like?" Malia met his gaze. "And I'm not going to just give it up and take the chance of a pregnancy when I know he'll walk away. So, stop, and tell Louris and the rest to stop. I have enough on my mind without needing to worry about something that's never going to happen."

"Very well, then."

Malia nodded as they stepped off the elevator and stayed silent down the corridor. "When are we docking?"

"We enter the Halifax system in four minutes. Don't forget, you cannot leave his quarters until we are out of the system which could be up to seven days."

"Seven days? I thought we were dumping off."

"We are, but there's also an important meeting going on, and we must wait for the other party to show up if they're not there already. Then we have to get out of the system, before you can step foot outside the door."

Malia met his gaze when he turned, a door swooshed open, and he motioned for her to enter. Her gaze narrowed. "Lose the smile before I smack you."

"Come on Lia, it won't be that bad."

Her gaze went to the divan and headed toward it, setting her small bag down on the floor as she sat. "Well, I guess it's comfortable enough."

Edmunds chuckled. "There's a cot set up for you in the sleeping quarters."

"Yeah, ah, no. I'm not sleeping in the same room as him, Edmunds. So go get the pillow and blanket and let me be."

"As you will."

Malia grabbed the items when he came back, her gaze going up when Ruskin's voice came over the intercom to the room, asking if the package was situated.

"Yes, sir, the item has been delivered to your chambers."

"Good, we're entering the Halifax system in three, two, one. Edmunds to the bridge."

"On my way, Commander."

Malia nodded her head when he did, her gaze on him as he stepped out the door. "Wonderful," she snorted and flopped down on the cushions. "I've been demoted from a person to a package."

*

Nolan stepped into his quarters, the room dark, and closed his eyes for a moment before opening them to transition from light to dark and spotted her outline on his divan. Edmunds had told him; she was against using the cot in his bedchambers. He understood. He didn't want to be any closer to her than he had to. He didn't know what the Gods were up to, signing them, but it had to be a damn joke of some kind. Heading towards his chamber, he stopped when she mumbled and turned, his cock hardening with the sight of the blanket falling, baring her leg. His eye twitched as he turned, his chest rose, pecs hitting his shirt as the door shut behind him. "Damn I don't need this."

*

"No, but you need to listen to what is being told to you."

Nolan's gaze narrowed.

"Don't narrow your gaze at me, Nolan Seager Ruskin."

Nolan met his mother's gaze as his brow lifted. "Mother, you don't seem to understand the issues here."

"Oh, I'm sorry, did you sign with this girl?"

"That has already been answered." He growled.

"Then you have your answer. Now do not upset the Gods, Nolan. Everything will work out as it should, so do not let that stop you. On another note, I am heading back to Paseon on the moon cycle, council is breaking for the life-giving season. Will your father and I be seeing you and your mated one for the festivities?"

She knew the answer, she just wanted him to confirm. "Yes Mother, I will see you and father for the festivities."

"Very well then, Vestor out."

The moment his mother's image disappeared, his smile dropped, as he hit the button to open his door. He knew he wasn't fooling her. "Taltz!"

"Commander?"

Nolan waited until he was in the doorway, the door shutting behind him. "Has anyone spoken with the Vestor?"

Taltz's hands went up. "Whoa man, not me, and I know no one on this ship would dare overstep you, even to the prime. Aunties scary and everything, but your crew is loyal, as you know."

"Then how in the frakin fires of Kelsar does she know about Lia and me signing?"

"Whoa, what? You and Li...I have no idea. Frak, I can't keep up with her on a good day. I don't know Nolan, seriously, if I did, I'd tell you, you know that."

Nolan lifted his hand. "Yeah, I know. It just stuns the shit out of me, how she knows before I tell her."

"Are we sure she's not a seer?"

Nolan turned, his gaze narrowed, they'd had this conversation before.

Taltz, stepped back, hands up. "Just saying."

Nolan shook his head as he glanced at his desk, his eyes going to the right. "No, she would have told me by now," and sighed. "Damn it, Taltz!" his gaze went to the door as it swooshed closed. "Bring her home, yeah, that's what I wanted to do. Bring her home and set her up as my Mated One in my dwelling. By the Gods, how did I get into this? I never should have deviated from going after Drago."

CHAPTER 5

MALIA'S LIP LIFTED WITH a snarl when Nolan stepped into his quarters. "When are we leaving?"

"After my meeting."

"Which is when? We've been here for eight days."

"I know all right!"

Her gaze narrowed as he sat on a chair, while his hand ran through his short, cropped hair.

"This isn't any easier on me than it is on you, but I have orders."

"Orders from who? You're a damn bounty hunter."

"My mother." He growled.

"Awww, isn't that cute. You're still taking directions from your mommy."

Nolan's gaze narrowed as he met hers. "My mother is a Prime. When she gives an order, you listen."

Malia nodded. "I've heard about the Prime's of Paseon. Very mystical, intelligent individuals." Grinning, she leaned forward. "Obviously, you take after your...father's side." Her nose crinkled with her smile.

"I'm going to spank your ass."

"Ha! Try it! Then again, don't. I might like it and that would just get us in trouble." She kept his gaze, smiling. "You do realize the longer we hold out, the worse it'll be for the both of us."

"The Gods do not control my life."

Her gaze stayed on him as he jumped up and started pacing. "Nolan," she whispered. "Just dump me off."

"No."

"Then what are you going to do with me? Lock me up, never to leave this ship, never to see anyone, but always have the agonizing pain ripping through my system every time we come in contact? How fair is that, not only to me, but to yourself? If you leave me on a secure world, at least we won't have the signs making it difficult for us."

"I. Said. No."

His whispered words had her gaze meeting his back as he left his quarters. "Then I'll have to leave on my own." Her chest rose with a deep breath as her eyes shut. What most didn't know about the people from her planet, was yes, their eyes shimmered when a mate was located. If the mating did not take place and they stayed close, she'd lose her eyesight little by little, and it was already starting to affect her. "Damn it."

*

The moment Nolan walked out of his sleeping quarters, Malia sat up, head down. "Can you please have Louris stop by today?"

"Yeah, sure, you, okay?"

"Yep, I just wanted to ask her something. I shouldn't use the intercom right now, right?"

"Yeah, right."

"Okay, thanks."

"Sure."

Lia waited. She knew he was waiting for her to look up at him, but she'd be damned. Oh, her eyesight was affected all right. She couldn't damn well see. The hell.

It was almost dinner time when Louris came in. "The Commander said you wanted to ask me..." her gaze went wide when Lia lifted her head. "By the Goddess."

"I'm all right."

"All right, hell. Why didn't you tell Nolan there was something wrong?"

Malia felt Louris, tilted her head and noted the light from the beam shining into her eyes.

"We need to get you to the med bay."

"I know what's wrong. Most outside of the Desolate Three don't."

"Well, by the Gods, fill me in."

"When we find our signed mate, and do not mate, our sign becomes our penance for not listening to the Gods."

"Computer, get me Commander Ruskin."

Malia grabbed for her. "No, no don't."

"He has to know, if not now, then at the meal when you can't find the damn fork."

"Commander Ruskin is on the bridge," came the computerized voice.

"Code Red – Louris 714."

"Louris, Louris, stop." Malia cried.

"Louris, what the hell, I'm in the middle of..." The growl of his tone had Lia sitting back.

"I need you in the makeshift med unit now, Commander!"

"On my way. Ruskin out."

Malia sat quiet until the faint swish of the door and his footsteps came running in.

"Well, I see no blood, so what the ..."

Malia lifted her gaze, he stopped and Louris started. When they began talking about her as if she wasn't there, she finally spoke up. "Stop it! The both of you, just stop."

"Is it reversable?" Nolan asked.

"Does it matter?" she choked.

"By the Gods, yes, it matters Lia! I'll not have you..."

"And I'll not have you screw me just because! We both know you want nothing to do with me. Thanks, but I don't need a pity fuck!" Her chest rose rapidly, hitting her shirt, nostrils flared as her eyes watered. Curling up on to the sofa, she hid her head. "Just leave me alone." Her voice weak even to herself.

"Taltz, stay with her. Louris, with me to the med chamber."

"I don't need a damn babysitter! It's not like I can escape now anyways." She waited until they left. "Jerk."

"Really?"

"Oh, you're still here. Go away, Taltz."

"Can't do that. I have my orders."

"Then take me to the closest cruiser and program a secure world into it for me and let me leave."

"Can't do that either Lia, you know, number one, he'd never approve that, two, I don't feel like getting my ass kicked, and three, well, all of the above."

"Piss off." She mumbled as she hugged the pillow, listening to his soft chuckle.

*

Nolan glanced down as his father spoke.

"Do you feel for her, other than the intense need for a mating?"

"Yes." Sitting down, he met his father's gaze. "She's smart and funny. She has morals and hasn't been that blindsided by what happened to ruin her or make her hard against everything." He sighed. "I never thought the signs would hit me so quick or hard."

His father laughed. "I know exactly what you mean Nolan. The day I met your mother at the festival, I balked at the signs as well. I was just there on holiday from my recent mission and wanted fun, not a mate. The Gods want us to be with our mate. We're very lucky to have the signs."

Nolan nodded. "I know. But she'll never believe me now. I've made it perfectly clear; I want nothing to do with her or the signs."

"Then you'll have to convince her son. Toss her some of that Ruskin charm."

Nolan snorted. "She'd toss it right back at me and knock out an eye."

His dad hooted. "Ha! I like her already!"

"All right, thanks Dad. I'll talk to you later."

"Yes, later. Your mother told me you're coming home for the festivities and bringing her home with you. Mayhap you'll have some good news for her before your arrival."

"We'll see. Thanks Dad, Nolan out." Nolan turned to the door as his father's image faded from sight. His steps slowed and he stopped right before his door. He'd been running, taking her as a mate, the moment her words came back truthfully from his helmet. He was attracted to her, and he liked her. Damn, she was just as pissy as he was on some things, and pride was the biggest. He was in line for a promotion. Having a mate wouldn't be so bad; she could come with him while on ship or stay at his home on Paseon. Louris said he had seven days, from what she could tell, until the blindness became permanent. His chest rose with a large breath. He hadn't had to woo a woman in years, once they saw his rank and learned he owned his ship, they fell right into bed.

Nolan snorted. It was not going to be that easy with Lia, especially after the way he'd treated her. Stepping up, the door swooshed open, and he stepped in to see Taltz sitting on a chair and Lia sleeping on the sofa. "How is she?"

"She's all right, been sleeping for about an hour."

Nolan nodded. "Thanks."

"No worries. However, I wouldn't let her near the shuttle bay. She wanted to take off for a secure planet."

"Yeah, figured she'd want to."

"All right, then. I'm out-oh and she wasn't happy to have a babysitter."

Nolan chuckled. "Better that than having her trying to find the shuttle bay and ending up in the trash shoot."

"Right."

"Oh, and you two are just hilarious." Lia said as she lifted her head. "Did you bring me dinner, Commander?"

"No, I brought you something better."

"Oh yeah, I don't smell anything, and I'm hungry."

Nolan nodded at Taltz as he headed to the door, before sitting beside her. "May I ask you something?"

"Sure."

Nolan's gaze on her as she sat up. Her eyes were glazed white. "If I hadn't been such an..."

"Ass."

"Yeah, okay, we'll go with that, besides my mother agrees with you. If I didn't fight the mating signs so hard, would you have gone along with them?"

"I guess so. I mean, the Gods give us the signs for a reason, to let us know we're in the presence of our true mate. Would I like to get to know you before a mating takes place? Of course! No matter how hot we're feeling for each other."

"It shocked the shit out of me."

"You and me both, Commander. I've been on my own, fighting for my survival, and had only myself to count on. I don't trust anyone and suddenly, my eyes are glowing, Kegels are clenching and I'm all hot and bothered, and all you have to do is look at me."

Nolan glanced down. "Trust is earned, not given lightly. I'm glad you understand that, Malia." He sighed as he hung his hands between his legs. "I'm not an easy person to be with, Lia. I am a hard-nosed, by the book bounty hunter. I have a crew who counts on me, and I need to make sure they get back to their families safely." He glanced over when she lay her hand on his arm.

"I understand Nolan. All of it. My aunt told me I needed to listen to my guides before she jumped the expanse. The truth is, I did. I was on Scurn III, because I listened. My guides gave me help when I least expected it, and then they brought me to you, and in case you haven't noticed. I'm not the easiest person to be near as well. I'm stubborn and don't take orders well. I'm always looking for an escape route no matter what room I'm in. The last four years have been hell. Living on Kelsar would have been easier."

"Yes, but they've made you the female you are now, and I respect you and everything you've had to go through to prove your innocence."

Malia tilted her head and he turned, his gaze on her. "Malia." His hand lifted to cup the side of her face. "I never wanted to hurt you, you know I'm attracted to you, and as we've never had mates, it's going to take getting used to. I haven't had to answer to another person for my personal life in a very long time."

"Are you going to treat me differently after we have sex? I don't want you to be intimate with me just because you feel bad, due to my eyesight. You're not going to change your mind about having me as a mate, are you?"

Nolan leaned forward, touching his forehead to hers. "When we do have sex, it will not be for pity or because we must. It will be because we want each other, and if you feel anything but fully satisfied, then I'm lacking and as Taltz would say, lost my mojo, and no, once we mate, that's it, girl, you're stuck with me." He chuckled kissing her softly, smiling when she did and backed up when the notification went off that someone was at the door. "Dinner's here."

CHAPTER 6

MALIA TOOK HIS HAND and let him lead her into the sleeping chamber. She'd only been through it, to use his personal relieving room and to clean.

"You're fidgeting."

"I'm nervous."

"How about we just cuddle tonight? You do like to cuddle, don't you?"

Lia sat on the bed. "I do and you smell good, so that helps." She smiled.

"Smart ass."

Lying down, his arm her pillow, they spooned, and she enjoyed his warmth as he wrapped his large body around her. "Nolan, what was your favorite thing to do as a child and with whom?"

"Camping with my father. He's in the military, so when he was home, it was something we'd do every time. Even after he became stationed to the planet, we'd go out, just the two of us, at least four times an annual cycle. You?"

"Mmm, I loved geode and gem hunting with my dad. We'd take off for days."

"Both of your parents are gone?"

"Yes, for quite some time now."

"I'm sorry."

Lia gripped his hand. "Thank you," she whispered.

*

Lia laughed at something Nolan said, they had just finished eating dinner and sat next to each other. "Nolan?"

"Hmm?"

"May I kiss you?" Her breath hitched when he moved closer.

"Most definitely."

Malia leaned in slowly. Her hand moved from his forearm, traveling up his bicep. Her hot breath hit her back as her lips softly touched his cheek. His hand cupped her jaw and she pressed into it. Tilting her head slightly, her nose brushed his, just as their lips touched, her intake of breath as his ran over her highly sensitized skin. A sound escaped her throat when his tongue ran along her bottom lip. "Nolan." She breathed heavily; tingles swam from her head along her spine.

The faint sweet taste of Rondalyn wine on her lips as he sucked the bottom one into his mouth gently. His name on her lips caused his cock to pulsate, pressing tight against his pants, as she leaned into him. Releasing the suction, he nibbled the lip softly, before sliding his tongue in to play with hers.

Lia moaned, every stroke of his tongue and duel with hers had her body vibrating with want.

"Commander, you're wanted on the bridge. Commander Ruskin to the bridge."

Malia leaned into him as he groaned at the computerized voice.

"Computer, put me through to the bridge." Nolan stated as he lowered his head to the nook of her neck.

"Bridge."

"Edmunds, what the hell is going on?"

"Sorry Commander, we have a Federation officer on board with a message for you."

Nolan sighed as he leaned back. "Show them to my office, I'll be there shortly, Ruskin out."

Lia leaned in as his thumb brushed across her cheek.

"I'm sorry, Lia. I have to go."

"I understand."

"I'll be back as soon as I can."

Malia chuckled as he rose off the sofa. "Nolan, you have a job to do, go do it, I'm fine." Smiling, when he came in real fast for a kiss and then he was gone.

*

Nolan's eye twitched as he stepped off the lift; he'd had to rearrange himself coming up. Damn it, this better be good.

"Commander on the bridge." Edmunds called out.

Nolan's lip lifted and eyes narrowed as he headed to his office, his gaze on the back of a Federation officer. He waited until the door closed. "This better be good." His jaw tightened when the man turned. "Korth, it's about fucking time."

Korth smiled. "Well, isn't that just the cheerful hello I've come to expect from you, Commander."

Nolan eyed him as he took an envelope out of his jacket.

"Now, I fully expect you to give this to Vestor Prime."

"Where the hell else do you think it's going to go? You know as well as I she'll have my ass in a sling if what she wants isn't delivered."

"Yes, your mom is quite the female."

"And you have the balls of a Greysfier hound, to just walk onto my ship. It is full of bounty hunters, you know."

"Yes, well, I just arrived and am on a tight schedule, so I didn't want to waste time to set up a meeting, figured I'd bring the info right to you."

"And if you've been sighted?"

"That has been taken care of, Commander. No one saw me come on and no one will see me leave."

Nolan shook his head. He didn't know how Korth did it, but he knew what Korth said was true. He probably had someone in the security rooms, making sure there was no footage of him on the station whatsoever. "All right, Korth. I have what you need to get to my mother. I'm sure you don't want to stay and have tea."

Korth laughed. "While that would be nice, I should take my leave."

Nolan gazed at him as he headed to the door.

"Oh, I almost forgot." Reaching into his jacket, he took out another packet and handed it to Nolan. "For you, Commander, and your mate, courtesy of Vestor Prime, and only because she is someone I adore."

Nolan lifted his eyes from the packet to Korth, who smiled. "With what Malia has already, everything in here should help you clear her, and don't worry about Vultag. Once he hits the prison system, he'll be dealt with for going against orders. Have a wonderfully boring life, Commander, except in the bedchambers."

Nolan glanced down at both packets, stored them in his desk, and walked out to the bridge. "Are we clear?"

"Yes sir, the officer is off the ship." Edmunds answered.

"Good, let's get the hell out of here." Sitting down in their chairs, the crew made ready to depart the station.

"So, I take it that was your meeting?"

"Yeah, it sure was. You're supposed to meet with Lia in the morning after your shift, right?"

"Yes, to go over avenues to find her former superior."

"I have something we need to look at." He met his gaze. "It just came into my hands. Let me know when we're out of the Halifax system," Nolan said as he rose and headed back to his office.

*

Malia smiled as Nolan placed her fingers on the inside of his elbow to lead her to Edmunds. "Nolan?"

"Hmm."

"Will you kiss me?"

Nolan glanced down with a smile as soon as he had her in the lift.

Lia gasped as he yanked her to him, his hand going behind her neck as the other pressed her lower back against his hard on. His mouth on hers, she met him, not slow like last night, but rushed and hot. "Oh." She smiled when he backed up, her nostrils flaring with his musk.

"You okay with that?"

"Ah, yes." She chuckled as he tucked her fingers back into his elbow crook when the doors opened.

Malia knew they were staring at her. "I, I don't know what to say." She whispered, the brush against her leg and a hand on her knee let her know Nolan was kneeling by her side.

"It's over, you don't need to run or hide anymore. Once we get this to the Federation, you'll be free."

"But, how?"

"Someone who adores my mother, dropped it off before we left the Halifax system."

Her lower lip trembled; tingles ran over her skin causing goosebumps. Tears ran down her face as sobs broke from her throat, and she leaned into Nolan when his arms went around her, dragging her down onto his lap. As he sat on the floor, she buried her face in the crook of his neck.

"It's all right, sweet." His hand ran over her hair and down her back.

Malia didn't know how long they had sat like that, but her sobbing had ceased, and she was enjoying being in his arms.

"Are you okay now?"

"Yes, I think so." Lifting her head, she drew back a bit. "Nolan, I want you to promise me something."

"Tell me what it is, and I'll let you know if I can."

"I want you to bring in Vultag,"

"Okay, I can take the warrant."

"And I want to be with you when you do."

"Now, that I'm not liking."

Her fingers squeezed his arms. "Please Nolan, you know what this means to me. I'll follow your every order and..."

"Really Lia, you think you can be that acquiescent?" Edmunds chuckled.

"Shut up, Edmunds."

"Just stating a reality."

"All right you two, that's enough. And I'll think about it," Nolan said quickly when Lia turned to him. "Lia, what we do is dangerous, you're not trained, and Vultag will not go easily."

Malia stood when he lifted her hand. "But..."

"I said, I'd think on it, now, let's leave it there and go grab some dinner."

Lia nodded as she gripped his hand and was about to argue when her stomach grumbled. "Oh, okay."

*

"What are you about?" Nolan smiled as Malia crawled over his lap, straddling him.

"I want to kiss you."

His hand lowered to her waist, and he set down his paperwork with the other before encircling her waist, to settle her on top of his cock. "How's your eyesight?"

"Mmm, it's coming back, I can see shadows. Louris said it's probably because we've been kissing and stuff."

"You told Louris we've kissed?" His gaze went to her lips.

"She said she could smell your musk on me and asked if we'd been intimate or mated."

Nolan snorted. "She knows we haven't mated; she was just reaching for info."

"How would she know?"

"Because once we mate and I orgasm inside you, my musk will mark you and all from Paseon will know we are mates. That way, no other male will approach you for sex." His hands tightened, pressing her against his hardness, his breathing picked up as her eyes closed and lips parted.

"Nolan."

"Hmm?"

"You, you said you wanted to put me against the wall and fuck my brains out."

"I did." He growled, knowing she noticed his dick flex with her words as she gasped, her breasts pushing against her shirt.

"Can we?"

His hands moved up her ribcage, cradling just under her breasts. "Wouldn't you rather wait until your sight comes back?"

"So, you can gaze into my eyes? Oh damn!" and leaned in when his thumbs ran across her hard nipples.

"Yes. I want to see your eyes glaze over with passion when I make you cum, as I'm pounding your pussy."

Lia gasped. "By the Gods, Nolan!"

His lips landed on her neck as he drew her close, nipping her with his teeth, a rumble escaping when she tilted her head, granting him complete access. His hand reached to the back of her neck, fingers entwining in her hair, and pulled down, her sigh of pleasure had his mouth on her neck, then her mouth, melting their lips together, his arms tightening around her as he took control. Her hands trembled as they lay on his chest, her heart thudding. Tingles ran from the base of his skull down his spine, right to his cock and pressed it hard against her warmth.

Her low sexy moan vibrated through him. Damn, he wanted to take her right here. His chest heaved as he backed up. "You're mine Malia."

Her body shook as he bit her neck. Her arms wrapped around his head. "Oh Nolan, please."

Nolan drew her into his embrace, his mouth going to her neck, and lifted her up, carrying her into his sleeping chamber. The moment he set her upon his bed, his knee between hers, and ready to lower her, his notification went off, and he groaned. Laying his forehead against hers. "Computer, who is it?"

"Vestor Prime, Commander."

"Put her through audio."

"Sorry Commander, she is requesting a vid call."

"By the Gods," he snarled. "Tell her I'm busy! Put her through to Taltz!" Sighing, he met Lia's opaque gaze. Her small hands rubbing his biceps. "I'm sorry, sweet. I have to get this."

"It's okay, Nolan, I understand."

Nolan leaned down and kissed her quickly, before straightening up. "Talk about a libido killer."

Malia chuckled softly. "We'll get our time."

Nolan's lips had just landed on hers, when Taltz came through the intercom. "By the Gods Taltz, tell her I'm on my friggen way!" meeting Lia's lips once more before he headed out.

Nolan met Taltz's gaze as he stepped onto the bridge and narrowed them, striding to his office. "Computer open channel to Vestor Prime."

"Commander, what was the hold up?

Nolan lifted his gaze to this mother.

"What's wrong, Nolan?"

"Do you really want to know?"

"Well, yes, I haven't seen that look on you for a very long time, are you all right, is everything well?"

"It would have been better. How do I say this so as not to offend my mother. You interrupted the making of your grandchild," He stated, crossing his arms. He'd never seen his mother blush, but once, when his father had whispered something in her ear at an event, and then they were taking their leave.

"Oh my, well, I apologize Nolan."

"Accepted, now what's so important?"

"Vultag escaped the team sent in to arrest him. He's on the run."

"So, he knows there's a warrant on his head?"

"Yes. Unfortunately, we had a mole in the division which has been dealt with. This happened less than an hour ago son."

"I want the warrant."

"It's already been transferred into your name; any information has been sent to Taltz and the ground team is awaiting your orders."

Nolan nodded, his mind going from pleasure to the hunt. "Mom, she wants to be there when we take him down."

"And you're against that?"

"I don't want her hurt," he said, meeting her gaze.

"I understand that Nolan, truly I do. But you must set aside your fears and believe in your mate. It's not easy, and if she does get injured, you cannot go ballistic. The fear that is running through you for her, runs through her for you. Your father and I still have a hard time when one of us goes on a mission. Granted, it's not as often as it was, as we're older, and though we have the ultimate trust in each other, we both know, if one of us is injured, we know we've done everything we could to not be hurt. Did I explain that correctly?"

"Yeah Mom, you did."

"All right, well good then." Yanking her jacket down she smiled. "Go get your warrant, Commander."

Nolan tilted his head and smiled. "Thank you Vestor Prime."

CHAPTER 7

MALIA HAD WOKEN UP with her sight restored-not fully. There were still white sparkles, but she could see, and she was late for the meeting. Stepping into the debriefing room with Taltz, she met Nolan's gaze as he turned. "I apologize for being tardy, Commander."

"Are you well?"

"Yes," she smiled. "My sight has all but returned, there are a few floaters swimming around, but Louris said they would dissipate." When he nodded, she went around him and took her seat at the table between Taltz and Edmunds. He had that emotionless mask on, she understood, they were getting ready to go up against someone who would rather kill you than look at you, and he wanted to make sure his crew knew exactly what was expected of them.

When Nolan came back to the sleeping quarters last night, he'd told her what had transpired. He told her she could be involved and made it clear she was to follow every single one of his orders without question, or else he'd leave her behind. She'd agreed and they held each other until she'd fallen asleep.

*

Malia glanced up with wide eyes when Nolan slammed his fist on the table. Edmunds told him the teams, and she was not on his. She would be on Edmunds'.

"Not happening." Nolan growled.

"Commander, let me explain." Edmunds asked.

Lia noticed the nerve on Nolan's jaw twitch as he nodded his head woodenly.

"Lia is your mate."

"Right, better for her to be with me, so I can keep an eye on her."

"And you will be keeping an eye on her, but not as close. Having her on my team will let Lia concentrate on what she must do, not how you are reacting to her. By the time we arrive at Cremon Three, you two will have mated. Sorry Lia, but we all know it's happening."

Malia nodded, her cheeks heated as Nolan glanced down, meeting her gaze.

"And we all know, once a Paseon mates, especially for the first annual cycle, males are more protective of their females. Not to mention your Kimeron half. If she sneezes, you may whisk her out of there, and that could damage the mission."

Malia kept Nolan's gaze, which softened, even though his jaw clenched. "I promise to listen to everything Edmunds tells me to do. If he tells me to abort and run, I'll do it."

"If you don't, I will spank your ass in front of this crew."

Her eyes widened as he nodded and continued with the meeting. The mercenaries Edmunds had mentioned before were in the room, she'd heard of the leader of this clan. His name was Vesper. He was as large as any male from Gruna and looked as mean, but if Nolan and Edmunds trusted him, she could too, especially seeing as how she'd be under his supervision during this mission. Louris was dragged on to the team with her, per Nolan. He wanted to make sure all areas were covered, should anything happen. Nolan changed the plans of Louris staying with Edmunds, she'd be dressed as a merc, standing with her.

Once they were in the lift, Malia turned to Nolan. "I thought the Jykar Mercs worked for Korth and the Hela Crime Organization."

"They have dealings with Korth as many entities do."

"Aren't you breaking protocol of some kind by working with outlaws?"

Nolan glanced down and met her gaze. "And you were what, before we cleared you, with Korth's help, I might add?"

Her gaze narrowed as his brow arched. "Do you have a habit of following the gray line?"

"I have a habit of following the truth and doing what's right."

"And that includes working with mercenaries?"

"I work with a lot of beings, Lia, and yes, I work with mercenaries on occasion. I am very good friends with several. As you also know, being a merc is approved by the Galactic Federation. Just because they push the legal lines close, doesn't mean they're bad. Vultag is listed as a shipping and exporting entity and look at his criminal activities."

"Yes, I understand what you're saying." She gasped as he lifted her to him, his mouth on hers, and rolled her hips against his hard on, sighing with his growl.

Malia wrapped her legs around his waist, he gripped her bottom, his mouth commanding hers, the taste of him invading more than her soul.

"Computer," he breathed as he stepped off the lift. "Do not bother me unless we're under attack, transfer all communications to Taltz, until further notice. Ruskin, Nolan, Commander, Code Furling 2401."

"Received, Commander."

Nolan met Malia's gaze as the door to his quarters shut behind them.

Malia's gaze widened. "Oh, Nolan, you, your canines are lengthening." *I didn't think Paseonians...*

His tongue filled her, her moans as he thrust his hard cock against her wet heat, his large hands, squeezing her thighs and ass as he made his way to the sleeping chambers.

"Half Kimeron." He stated as he laid her on the bed. "Strip."

The corner of her mouth tilted up as her hands went to her pants, his fingers there, helping her unbuckle them. Her shirt was off, and his dark head lowered. Her eyes closed on a moan as his lips wrapped around her nipple. Her hands went to his shirt, lifting it. His skin was hot to her caress, and then he rose, his gaze meeting hers.

"I don't like seeing scars on you." His tone low as he leaned down to kiss one on her shoulder. "No more, okay."

"Same goes for you." She caught a hint of his smile as she leaned up and kissed right below his left peck, moaning when it moved and lifted, taking his taut male nipple into her mouth. His breathing heightened as she nipped him with her teeth.

"Gods, woman!"

Malia chuckled as she wrapped her legs around him and tightened, bringing him to her, so he had to put his hands on the bed, on either side of her as to not fall on her, and she bit his peck. Her arms around his neck, she brought him close, as he slid one arm under her back, his mouth lowering and groaned as she urgently met him. Her hands roamed his amazing body; he was muscled and fit, not huge like men from Gruna or sleek muscled like the feline races, he was right in the middle, and she loved it. His muscles moved as her hands caressed.

His mouth moved down her neck, nibbling, biting, her sighs and moans had his cock twitching against her heat, and she lifted, pressing. He bit her shoulder when she rubbed her warmth along his length, her juices coating him. He knelt, his hands grasped her hips, bringing her to him, and buried his mouth between her legs.

Lia screeched, hands running through his short hair. "By the Gods, Nolan!" Her thighs widened to his tongue and lips. He nipped her clit, the tingles starting at the top of her head. "Oh, Nolan, Nolan." Ecstasy swam down her spine and jolted her senses. He sucked, and she cried out as her Kegels contracted, her body lifted, legs shook as lightning flew through her body. Never had she orgasmed like this, never.

Nolan lapped up her essence. The corner of his mouth lifted as her legs flopped to the bed. Lifting his gaze, her chest rose rapidly, her nipples pointing straight up as he pressed his tongue to her enlarged nub. Her body shook slightly, and he rose, his pants hitting the floor as he sprawled beside her and smiled as her eyelids fluttered. Her color had gone from sky blue to a dark sapphire. "Hello, beautiful."

Malia smiled, her lips swollen from his kisses and beard.

"You ready for more?" he asked as he leaned down, softly caressing her lips with his.

"Yes, oh!" When he lifted her to her knees to kneel in front of him, the strength of his body had her lips parting as she met his gaze. Her hard nipples rubbed against his chest, and she lifted her hands, settling them there, as his went from her waist to her ass, roaming over her heated flesh, as he moved closer. His hand lowered to her mound and she moaned when he applied pressure to her clit. Her nostrils flared with the scent of his musk. It was stronger than before, and she reached down, taking his thick cock in her hand.

Nolan groaned, his hand over hers, and squeezed hard as he stroked himself several times before removing her hands behind her back. "Not yet."

"But I want to touch you."

"Hmm, you will, just not yet." Her hips arched with a moan as he cupped her, his finger sliding into her warmth. "You're so wet baby, Gods." His thumb hit her clit and started rubbing. Turning her, so her back was to his chest, his mouth lowered to her neck, hand back to her mound. "Do not cum this time. When you feel your orgasm coming, tell me."

"Oh, okay."

"I mean it, Lia," his hot breath on her sensitive neck had her shivering. "If you cum without my allowance, I'll spank you."

"Oh, well, that kind of sounds...interesting."

Nolan smiled. "You think so, if I have to spank you for a punishment, not pleasure, I will not let you orgasm." He cupped her pussy, thumb strumming her clit.

"I, I don't think I'd like that."

"That's right, you wouldn't," he breathed, nibbling her ear. "I want to orgasm with you; our mating bond will be stronger. If I bite, don't be scared, it's the Kimeron in me, and because I want to."

Her entire body shook. "Please, Nolan, I, I want you to do all of it, by the Gods you make my body hot and tingly and..." Her head leaned back against his shoulder, his other hand moving from her hip to her nipple.

Lia cried out with pleasure as he surged into her from behind. He stretched her; his thickness drove her crazy, his fingers found her clit and she was about to topple over. "Nol... Nolan."

"Hold."

Breathing heavily, her Kegels tightened around his cock with every deep thrust, her head lying back on his chest, body shaking. "Please Nolan, please."

His hot breath on her ear. "Release for me." He whispered, pinching her clit, and groaned as her muscles clenched around his shaft. His teeth sank into the curve of her neck and met her in euphoria and the bonding sync. Every memory from her early years, her wounds, the agony of being on the run, and the knowledge that she had seen his memories, childhood and pains, flashed through his mind, as their climax intensified, Nolan raised his head in a shout, as his seed shot out deep within her warmth.

Malia's chest rose rapidly, her body trembled, every nerve within her was alive and moving as wetness dropped down her cheeks.

"Why are you crying my sweet?" he asked as he lay them down, spooning her. "Tell me you're all right." His arms wrapped around her, drawing her as close as he could.

"You didn't hurt me Nolan. I swear." His warmth blanketed her, his fingers brushed her hair away so he could see her eyes flutter open to meet his. "I've never felt like that. The orgasm and then, the, the bond. I never thought, it would be so...intense."

Nolan drew the cover over them and held her closely as her body shuddered. "It's my Kimeron. Paseonians don't bond like that. I should have explained it more in depth."

"It was quite awesome, just a little overwhelming."

Nolan glanced down, her eyes closed and breathing even. Slipping his leg between hers, he held her as his eyes fluttered, the silence around him beckoning him to sleep.

CHAPTER 8

"COMMANDER, ON THE BRIDGE." Taltz called out.

Nolan shot him a glance as the shift change members came on deck. "Debrief."

"We are twenty-hours from Pantu. The teams are ready for the mission debrief at the eighteenth hour. All systems are running normally. No issues or anomalies. Oh, except one."

Nolan turned to meet his gaze.

"The Prime, and you know whom I'm referring to, wanted to know why every time she tried to contact you, it came to me. She was, extremely and I say that in the nicest way possible, frustrated."

Nolan's gaze narrowed as Taltz grinned. "And you told her what?"

"That you were busy."

"And she stopped when you said that?"

"You were in the middle of making her a grandchild, so unless the planet was on fire or under attack, you were not to be bothered."

The corners of his mouth lifted. "And she?"

"You know, I've never seen Auntie blush before," He chuckled. "She said, when you were free to make contact."

Nolan nodded. "Have a good rest, we'll see you at shift end. Edmunds, make sure all final arrangements are made and things are in order for the mission debrief. It appears I have a call to make." Rising, he headed toward his office.

*

Nolan had her to the wall, his forearms under her thighs, palms on her ass. "You know I'm going to fuck the shit out of you, right?"

"Please do," she breathed as her mouth crashed down on his.

He opened to her urgency, an urgency that streamed through them both. They'd just come back from a short debrief of the mission for any updates. He didn't like putting her in harm's way. Didn't like it before they had mated, and sure as shit didn't like it now that she was his. His, in every way. His hand lifted and threaded through her hair, grasping it. He'd found out last night, she liked a bit of a rougher touch, and he was fine with that. Paseons and especially Kimerons, could be very rough when they mated.

"Please, Nolan." Her pelvis ground against his rigid dick. She'd opted to wear one of the Paseonian dresses which were free flowing, his hands slid underneath over her heated flesh.

She wasn't wearing any undergarments, sighing raggedly, he tore open his pants, his erection jutted free and guided it to the very edges of her swollen flesh. He was so damn hard, and she was wet, so beautifully wet for him. Nudging between her lips, the tip of his cock entered her, and she moaned, trying to lower herself onto him. He played with her, inching in and out, sucking on a hard nipple until he had her trembling.

"Nolan, fuck me!" Her hands grasped onto his short hair, and he rammed inside her, his girth filling her up completely, her shriek of pleasure and surprise as her tightness surrounded him.

"Gods, my sweet."

"Oh, I know, I know." Grabbing his head, she invaded his mouth, her tongue dueling with his, until he took over and she reveled in his dominance. Her hands clawed at him, as he broke the kiss. He quickened his thrusts, the glide and plunge of his hard flesh inside her, stroking her until her groans became moans and her body started zinging. "Oh, Nolan, I feel it."

"Hold, until I give leave." He met her gaze, her lids heavy with desire, lips plump from his assault on them, damn she was sexy, and she was all his. His lip lifted with a growl, and he hammered between her thighs, tightening his grasp on her hair. "Open your eyes."

"But, oh."

"Keep them open and on me, I want to see you."

"Nol..."

"Hold it." He growled. He could feel her pussy contracting on him. She was so ready and holding back for him, for his word. She trusted him. He observed her stunning blue eyes as they began to darken with her passion. He thrust hard, right to her womb. "Now! Release for me."

Her body exploded as he buried deep again, hitting the top of her womb and she cried out as she kept his gaze. His own roar filled her ears and she could feel his seed ejecting into her. His eyes changed and canines lengthened, and when he bit the nerve between her neck and shoulder, her eyes widened with a scream as her insides clenched around him, spasming. Her body shook and he held her, his plunges hard and deep but not hitting her cervix as he rode the second wave with her.

Nolan held her to the wall, his mouth nuzzling her jaw and neck. "Are you all right?"

"Completely boneless."

He chuckled as he pushed away and made his way to the bedroom as she drifted off.

*

Nolan's gaze narrowed as Malia came out of the female quarters dressed in the clothing she'd been wearing the day he captured her.

"Why are you looking so grumpy?"

"You know why." He held her gaze as she walked to him, her arms going around his waist, and he wrapped his around her, bringing her close, his cheek on the top of her head.

"Nolan."

"Hmm?"

"I want you to take a large breath and let it out slowly."

He did. "No help."

"I'll be fine. I won't leave your sight. Louris is going to place the communicator and tracker as well as finish out my appearance. She'll be right there by my side. Vesper is your friend; he knows you'll beat him senseless should anything happen to me."

"Still doesn't help." He mumbled, his gaze meeting hers when she backed up, her smile faltered, and eyes lowered. "Lia, what's wrong?"

"I, I know we're mated, and you like me, but..."

Nolan smiled as he grabbed her to him. "Look at me." He waited until she did just that, his hand lifted to cup the side of her face. "You, I don't know how you did it, Malia Bash'ar Ruskin, but, I don't just like you."

"You don't?"

"No. I like you, like you, really like you, woman! You have brought out feelings in me I haven't had since I was a boy, just having feelings for the first time. I don't speak of what I feel much. Neither do you, I may add." He cupped the other side of her face and met her gaze. "Lia, you are my heart mate."

Her lips wobbled. "Oh Nolan." She whispered; her eyes fluttered when he softly brushed his lips across hers. "You are my heart mate."

"Hey Commander, are we ready to get Lia ..."

"I believe they are having a moment, Louris." Taltz chuckled.

Nolan smiled, ignored his crew and softly kissed her, not once, but several times. Before he backed up. "Okay?"?"

Lia nodded. "Okay, grumpy."

"I'm not grumpy anymore." He chuckled.

"No, but you will be. You will be." She smiled.

"Is that a warning?"

Lia turned and smiled at him. "Possibly."

Nolan's brow lifted as she grabbed Louris' arm, and they took off. "Not liking that."

"Ah, it's all good," Taltz chuckled. "So, I take it you two are getting along?"

"Yep."

Taltz slapped him on the back. "She'll be fine. Not only are Vesper and his mercs, but we are watching her six. Besides, she's a smart and intuitive female."

"She is. Still doesn't help with me wanting to rip out anyone's jugular who comes near her right now."

"Ah man, that's the Kimeron in you."

"Oh sure, blame it on the feline. You wait until you sign. I'm going to drop whatever I'm doing to come tell you to get your Paseon under control." His lip curled, they glared at each other and belted out in laughter.

"Let's go, Commander. We have a bounty to get."

*

Malia heard his growl and 'by the fires of Kelsar' through the communication device when she stepped out onto the ground from Vesper's shuttle. Louris grabbed her arm, tossed her hood up over her head, and kept her behind Vesper. "Hush." She whispered. She knew he wasn't going to be happy with what they had done. Not only had Louris planted the communication device and tracker in her, just under her ear that all his crew had, they had splattered dried blood, synthetic of course, and dirt over her face and clothing to make it look like she had fought a good fight. Her dark blonde hair was back in a ponytail, with pieces hanging out in different places. Louris even had another tracker on her just in case, in the form of a necklace with a Tamonian jade amulet.

"What in the hell is this Vesper, what do you want?" a male voice boomed.

Her insides froze and she tensed. Even after all these years, his voice could stop her still.

Vesper laughed. "I wouldn't be so hostile, Vultag, as I have something or should I say someone, you may want."

"The fuck are you talking about?"

Lia stepped forward when Louris nudged her arm. Although her hands were behind her back in cuffs, she could escape at any time, and she blinked as the hood was tossed back, lifting her head.

"What the fuck, you're dead!"

Malia watched as Vesper shot his hand out, stopping Vultag from advancing and narrowed her gaze.

"Is she?" Vesper said, turning to meet her gaze. "Boy I'll have to give my crew a raise, that vid came out awesome! Looks like she's breathing fine to me, although a little beat up. Got to give her credit though. She's a fighter." He winked, then turned back to Vultag. "How much?"

"Two hundred thousand credits."

Vesper laughed, crossing his arms over his chest. "Please, we both know you can do better than that."

"Five hundred thou."

His lips pursed out. "Keep talking."

"How much more do you want?"

"Well with what she has on you," he stated, lifting the small data reader she'd had tucked into the handle of her brush. "I'm thinking five hundred thousand for each of my crew members who had the pleasure of her capture. That's six total. So do the math Vultag."

"That's, that's three million credits!"

Lia's gaze narrowed as spittle flew from his mouth. He was such a disgusting pig.

"Oh, trust me, we're worth every credit." Vesper grinned.

"I'm not paying that! Not for that little whore!"

"Hey, I take offense to that! Just because I wouldn't sleep with you, doesn't make me a whore, you fucker!"

Vesper turned sideways to glance down at her. "My, my Malia, that's no way for a lady to talk."

Vultag snorted. "Lady, my ass."

Vesper grinned. "I have it on very good authority, she's only been with two men. Now about that pay out."

"I'm not paying shit. She's mine, I want her, now."

Lia's gaze widened when Vultag, elbowed Vesper aside, headed right to her, then he was yanked back. Shit, Vesper did not look happy.

"Wrong, she's mine." Vesper growled. "Don't make this difficult, Vultag. With what she was able to get on you, I can fuck you up right now and toss you to a Galactic Federation holding site. You will go before trial, you will stand for the murder of her former boss, you know, the one you killed personally, shot to the back of the head he was on his knees." Vesper tossed him a smaller data holder. "Here. Look for yourself and decide. You have two minutes. After that, the deal's off. She's damn good at going undercover. I may keep her, after she pays off her debt to me, that is," he smiled. "And make her a member of my crew and clan."

Malia noticed Vultag's hand shaking as he took the data holder and inserted it into his wrist reader.

"Oh, and you really shouldn't get drunk if it makes you spill all your deep secrets." Vesper said and turned to face her as two of his men came forward. One whispered in his ear, and the other watched Vultag closely.

Lia's eyes followed as Vesper strode to Louris and whispered something in her ear. They obviously didn't want Vultag to hear, and wondered what was going on. She couldn't turn and ask Louris outright, as that would break character.

"Where the fuck did you get this!"

Malia's gaze whipped to Vultag as he stomped over to her, his face red and puffed as Vesper and his man stepped in front of her.

"Well?" Vesper asked.

"Where the fuck did you get this?"

"Her, and there's a lot more, that was only a snippet. You know when you kill someone, say her boss, you shouldn't go around declaring it for everyone to hear, right?"

"I was drunk."

"Ah yes, but on three of the others, you are not. You are as sober as we are standing here today. So again, Vultag, are you going to meet my price for her and her evidence or not?"

"You killed him." Lia whispered, all turning to look at her. Edmunds had said having him admit it straight out would be great. "You killed Lartis and probably Zennia too, because I can't find her. You killed them and blamed it on me because I wouldn't sleep with you."

Vultag sneered. "You little bitch. I sold Zennia to the highest bidder; she wouldn't give you up. Even after I shot that worthless piece of shit Lartis through the brain in front of her, she wouldn't give you up."

"She didn't know where I was! I ran!" Lia moved forward before Louris grabbed her arm. "I ran you, bastard, because you killed him! Where is she, where's Zennia!"

"I sold her to Ranelius!"

Tingles of fear ran through her. "You sold her to a slaver!"

"He's an importer and exporter, and you Malia, if you'd just opened your friggen legs, she wouldn't be in slavery somewhere and Lartis wouldn't be dead."

"You son of a bitch!" Lia struggled with Louris and made headway to Vultag when Vesper stepped in front of her.

"Now, now, now my dear. Don't get so upset. You've lived on the run for the past four years, you know it happens. Now back to you Vultag. Are you paying my price or not? No more stalling. I have a schedule to keep. Yes or No?"

"Fine! Yes, I'll pay it, I want all evidence she's collected, you keep none, no copies, nothing."

Vesper smiled. "Fine, fine. Now send the credits to this link."

Malia took deep breaths to calm down. Louris had squeezed her arm and laid a hand on her back to comfort her but for now that's all she could do. Tears welled as she thought about the woman who had befriended her, had cared for her. She would have Nolan find Zennia and free her. She glanced up when Vesper stepped up to her.

"Well, my dear, I'm sorry to say our paths do not seem inclined to stay crossed. A shame, really. I was kinda hoping he wouldn't want to pay. You'd be an asset to my clan, and a very good friend of mine, who I know would love to get you in his bed." He winked. "But alas, he's paid my price." Lia walked with him to Vultag and stood there when he let her arm go. "She's all yours, Vultag."

Lia met Vultag's gaze.

"How do I know you'll turn everything over to me?"

Vesper laughed. "Between the both of us, I'm the honest one. You'll get your evidence, now my crew and I are out."

Malia kept Louris' eye as they backed up to the shuttle and entered, closing the door behind them. Her breathing became rapid as she turned to Vultag, who was watching the shuttle take off. She lowered her shoulder, tackling him. Her hands released and came forward hitting him. "You son of a bitch!" Her fist hit his head as they went down. This wasn't part of the plan, she was supposed to run, and Nolan would step in, but she couldn't help herself. Rising, she hit him again and again. She heard boots stomping in the distance and talking on the internal communication device but ignored it as she kept swinging.

"Malia Bash'ar, you're under arrest for murder." Nolan stated as he grabbed her by her arms and lifted her back.

"Get away from me, Space Warrior!" Her feet kicked out, hitting Vultag in the stomach. "If I'm going down for murder, let me kill him!"

Nolan cuffed her and brought her back up against his chest. "Lia, calm down, sweet." He whispered.

She heard him through her communication device, not out loud, as Edmunds and the team came forward to arrest Vultag.

"Ornius Vultag, you have a warrant on you for the murder of...Commander, he's wanted in conjunction with the warrant out on Bash'ar."

"How's that..."

"He killed him!" Malia cried. "He killed Latius, not me." She had to get control. Taking a deep breath, she leaned back onto Nolan and closed her eyes breathing deeply. "The data holder up his sleeve, it has everything to clear me..."

"Shut up you bitch!" Vultag swore.

"It clears me," she cried. Why the hell was she crying? She never cried.

"We'll clear this out on board. Get him and let's go."

His arm went around her waist, holding her and firing his jet pack. She'd never flown like this, and it was exciting and scarry at the same time. Once they landed near his shuttle on the other side of the clearing, Nolan helped her to the seating area, as they took Vultag to the holding cells.

Once Vultag was out of earshot, he knelt in front of her, taking his helmet off. "Are you all right?" She'd been silent and unresponsive. Not like her at all. "Malia, sweet, are you all right?"

"Yes."

"Awww my dearling," he whispered when she lifted teary eyes.

Malia burrowed onto him as he took her into his embrace, sitting on the chair next to her as his crew worked around them, he released the cuffs. Her small hands wrapped around his waist. "Nolan."

"Hmm?"

"I'm free, really, really free of him and, and running."

"You are. Taltz confirmed he has everything on vid. Vultag is going down, my heart, and you, well, you are mine."

Malia lifted her head and met his gaze. Her fingers glided down the side of his face. "As you are mine, Space Warrior." She leaned in, his lips a bare inch away when Louris rang out. 'Did you tell her?'

Lia blinked as Nolan lifted his head, eyes narrowing at his head medical officer. "Tell me what?"

"Bug off, Louris." Nolan growled.

Malia turned her head to see Louris grinning with Edmunds standing by her. "What?"

"I will tell you tonight, when we're alone."

"We're all family here." Louris chimed.

"Shut up, Louris. Edmunds, do something with her, will you?"

"What do you think he's going to do?" Louris asked, hand on hip.

"Well, you're looking hot in that merc gear." Edmunds grinned.

Lia looked from them as Edmunds wiggled his eyebrows at Louris, whose lip lifted with a growl. "I'm not understanding." She said as two more crew members came in and sat down with smiles.

"When you were brought aboard Vesper's shuttle, they do scans like we do."

"Okay, and?"

"And...you're carrying."

CHAPTER 9

MALIA FROWNED. "CARRYING WHAT? You made me leave weapons on board, so I didn't blow Vultag to pieces." Her gaze whipped over to Edmunds when he slapped his palm on his forehead and Louris groaned. "I don't get it. I don't have a bomb on me or anything."

"No, but you have one in you." Taltz laughed over her communicator.

"For the love of Kimeron," Nolan growled. "Will you all shut up!"

Lia turned back to Nolan as he ran his hand over the top of his head, his eye catching hers and stopped, looking straight at her.

"You, my heart, are with child."

Her lip went up with a frown. "With child," her gaze lowered to the right. "With, with..." and lifted wide eyes. "You, you mean, I'm pregnant?" His smile grew as they continued to stare into each other's eyes. "Oh, oh Nolan." She wrapped her arms around his neck. "We're going to have a baby."

"We are."

Lia backed up and started placing kisses all over his face until he laughed. "Nolan, Nolan, we're going to have a baby."

"I know, my heart." He chuckled, taking her face between his hands, lips lowered to hers kissing the dickens out of her as his crew exploded in cheers.

*

"What's wrong?"

Malia glanced over at Nolan. "I'm nervous."

"Yeah, about what?"

"Well, I'm going to be meeting your parents. What if they don't like me?"

Nolan and Taltz chuckled. They were sitting in the shuttle going from the space station to the planet of Paseon. "Auntie can be a bit intimidating."

"She's a Prime. Of course, she's intimidating, Taltz." Nolan grinned.

Lia whimpered. "That's what I'm saying. What if she doesn't like me? She's a Prime, I mean by the Gods."

Nolan drew her into his embrace. "Mom will like you, because I like you, because we signed, we're bonded, and you're carrying her grandbaby."

She sighed loudly as she leaned into him. "I hope so. I mean, no pressure or anything."

Malia stepped off the shuttle, her hand squeezing Nolan's as he greeted his parents. She came around to his side, her eyes widening, and she smiled. "Sherrin!" Letting go of Nolan, she ran to the female and hugged her. "I didn't know you'd be here. How are you?"

"Hello, my dear. I'm very well, how are you?" Sherrin smiled.

"Oh, by the Gods, I'm great! I'm pregnant. I'm going to have a baby." Taking her hand, she led her to Nolan. "This is my mate, this is Nolan, he's a bounty hunter and Commander. Nolan, this is Sherrin, she's my friend. Without her I don't know what I would have done this past annual season."

Nolan's brow lifted as Taltz chuckled. "Friend, huh?"

"Yes, yes." Malia's head tilted when he hadn't moved. "Nolan, are you okay? You don't have a problem with Sherrin, do you?"

He crossed his arms over his chest. "Problem, oh no, my sweet, I have no problem with her, in fact, I love her."

Malia's brows drew together. "Love. I'm not following."

"The Prime does it again." Taltz laughed. "I'm telling you man, she's a seer."

"Taltz, behave and stop calling me 'The Prime' before I take a switch to you," Sherrin stated as she met Taltz's gaze.

"I'm a grown man, Auntie, a warrior. Switch, really?" Her head tilted, and he lowered his arms from being crossed over his chest, his feet shuffling. "Okay, fine, damn it. Stop giving me the look."

"I'm lost." Lia muttered and met Nolan's smiling gaze when he drew her into his arms. "My heart, Sherrin is my mother."

Her gaze lowered to the left, then back to his. "Mother? Sherrin is your mom?" Turning, she met Sherrin's gaze as the woman smiled.

"I am, and welcome to the family, my daughter. Welcome home."

Malia wrapped her arms around Sherrin, as she took her within her arms and breathed deeply with a smile. Home. She hadn't had that in so long. "Sherrin."

"Hmm?"

"How did you know?" She smiled as she backed up. "About sending me to Scurn?"

Sherrin winked. "We'll go over that on another day. But for now, we need to plan your mating party and Nolan's promotion."

"Promotion?"

"Mother, I don't want anything big." Nolan interjected. "And sweet, this is my father. Admiral Nathanial Ruskin."

Lia moved her gaze from Nolan to the large man standing beside him. They looked so much alike. "It's a pleasure to meet you, sir."

Nathanial chuckled. "I like the greeting you gave to The Prime." He moved swiftly when Sherrin went to smack him. "A hug would be great, my daughter. I may be an Admiral, but I'm also Dad and a soon to be granddad. No sirs, Okay?"

Lia smiled as she gave him a hug. "Okay. So, what's this promotion?" She backed up, looking at Nolan. "You own your own ship; I didn't think bounty hunters had promotions."

"He's also a Commander in the Paseon fleet."

"That's why I'm a Commander, even though I own my own ship, sweet." Nolan said as he wrapped his arm around her. "I'll be promoted to Captain."

"Oh, Nolan, that's wonderful!" Malia stated, hugging him. "Wait, the Paseon fleet doesn't allow their mates to be on board with them."

"No, but I'm a bounty hunter by trade, so I can have you with me if you want."

Malia smiled, lifted her toes, and met his lips. "Good, because I don't think I'd like being away from you." Her eyes sparkled as she met his.

"Me either, my heart."

The End

About The Author

Hello wonderful Readers!

I have served as the Vice President of Communications and as Vice President of Programs for my former RWA chapter in Florida.

A Slave's Way Out, won The Torrid Title of the Year Award and made me a bestselling Author.

Writing is my passion and I look forward to it every day! Not so much the editing, LOL. ☺

I bow to my editor! She has her work cut out for her. ☺

Authors Note

Thank you for taking the time to read Space Warrior!
The Dragon King & The Shadow of The Bounty Hunter
sub-series in The Galactic Federation Series, is coming next.
As always,

Read Lots & Stay Spicy

C ~

**Love a book? Help others find it by leaving a review.
Authors will love you for it! Thanks!**

The Dragon King & The Shadow

When the Shadow, is called in to help the ally of a friend, Cambryn To'si lets her anger out as the family of the kidnapped takes matters his own hands.

King or not, she will not have someone inject themselves into her mission, whether they've signed to be mates or not. Dragon King, Nakoss Zeldar finds the female bounty hunter intriguing, even with a crime boss breathing down their necks and mentally controlling his people.

Steam pours out of Nakoss' nostrils when Cambryn declines his offer to mate. Unable to control the mating signs they're both feeling. Cambryn has another mission to complete before she can commit to any kind of relationship.

However, when Nakoss finds out she's meeting the same crime boss who's been after him, Cam has to break her black op and put her trust in a man she hasn't known very long.

Cover Reveal & Pre-order on: May 4, 2024
Book Release: June 1, 2024

The Galactic Federation Series:

The Galactic Federation Series is a combination of multiple spicy sub-series, within the same creative universe.

If you want sexy aliens, strong women and books that make you smile, and fan yourself all the way to the end, get this series today!

Each book in the Galactic Federation series can be read as a standalone and features a happily ever after. But you wouldn't go wrong to read The Retrievers sub-series first :-)

The Retrievers –

They are Retrievers. If something is stolen, they are hired to get it back.

They go in unseen and unnoticed, however getting out without being shot at, is another story.

They are one of the best teams in the Federation and are paid handsomely for their services.

They are family.

Bounty Hunters –

Join the Galactic Federation's bounty hunters as they track down the galaxy's fugitives,

take down the bad guys and locate their mates.

Destined to Mate

A feline mated to a werewolf?

As a Chimera, half lioness/half human, Alexis Xanthis, has never released the beast within. Until she meets Lykan Alpha, Morgan LeVey. Being near him triggers a powerful need to mate, but is Morgan strong enough to dominate her feline side and still handle the human half with a gentle hand? And will the powers that be allow it?

Undercover Lover Series

Being part of a special police unit, love was the last emotion
these four brothers thought they'd have to deal with.
Until they ran into the women who yanked their heartstrings.

www.ingramcontent.com/pod-product-compliance
Lightning Source LLC
Chambersburg PA
CBHW071233170626
46809CB00008BA/3046